W9-AMN-006

WITHDRAWN

Dear Parents and Educators,

Welcome to Penguin Young Readers! As parents and educators, you know that each child develops at their own pace—in terms of speech, critical thinking, and, of course, reading. Penguin Young Readers recognizes this fact. As a result, each Penguin Young Readers book is assigned a traditional easy-to-read level (1–4) as well as a Level (A–P). Both of these systems will help you choose the right book for your child. Please refer to the back of each book for specific leveling information. Penguin Young Readers features esteemed authors and illustrators, stories about favorite characters, fascinating nonfiction, and more!

Mo Jackson: Spike It, Mo!

LEVEL 3

LEVEL **J**

This book is perfect for a **Transitional Reader** who:
- can read multisyllable and compound words;
- can read words with prefixes and suffixes;
- is able to identify story elements (beginning, middle, end, plot, setting, characters, problem, solution); and
- can understand different points of view.

Here are some **activities** you can do during and after reading this book:
- One of the rules when adding -ing to words is, when a word ends with an -e, take off the -e and add -ing. With other words, you simply add the -ing ending to the root word. The following words are -ing words in this story. On a separate piece of paper, write down the root word for each word: swimming, resting, reading, standing. Next, add -ing to the following words from the story: get, serve, hit, spike, reach.
- Summarize: Work with the child to write a short summary about what happened in the story. What happened in the beginning? What happened in the middle? What happened at the end?

Remember, sharing the love of reading with a child is the best gift you can give!

*This book has been officially leveled by using the F&P Text Level Gradient™ leveling system.

For my sports-loving grandsons,
Jacob, Yoni, Andrew, and Aaron—D. A. A.

To Eden and Shiloh—S. R.

Penguin Young Readers
An imprint of Penguin Random House LLC
New York

First published in the United States of America by Penguin Young Readers,
an imprint of Penguin Random House LLC, 2022

Text copyright © 2022 by David Adler
Illustrations copyright © 2022 by Sam Ricks

Visit us online at penguinrandomhouse.com.

Library of Congress Cataloging-in-Publication Data is available.

Manufactured in Spain

ISBN 9780593352700

1   3   5   7   9   10   8   6   4   2

EST

SPIKE IT, MO!

by David A. Adler
illustrated by Sam Ricks

"Splash!" Mo Jackson says.

He swings his arms around.

He kicks one foot

and then the other.

"Splash! Splash!

I'm swimming."

"No! No!" his father laughs.

"You can't swim on the beach.

You can only swim in the water."

"I know that," Mo says.

"Let's *really* swim."

Mo runs to the water.

His father follows him.

Mo runs into the water.

"YIKES!" he screams.

"COLD! COLD! COLD!"

Mo runs out of the water.

People at the beach are resting.

People are reading.

"Dad, I'm bored."

His dad says, "Let's go for a walk."

"Watch out!"

A ball flies past Mo

and his dad.

A girl calls out,

"Throw it back!"

She and others are

standing by a net.

Mo's father says,

"It's a volleyball.

Hit it back."

Mo holds the ball with one hand.

He hits it with the other.

The ball flies high and far.

"Nice serve," the girl calls.

"We need two more for a game.

Do you want to play?"

"Oh, hi, Mo," the girl says.

"Hi, Eve."

"You'll be on my team," Eve says.

"You're my good-luck player."

Mo tells his dad,

"I know Eve from soccer."

Eve points to the players

on the other side of the net.

"That's Ed's team.

They serve first.

We get to hit the ball three times.

The third hit must go over the net."

Mo and his dad stand
in the back row.

"Here it comes," Eve calls.

The ball flies over the net
to the back row.

Mo's dad hits it to Eve.

She hits the ball over the net.

She hits it down and into the sand.

"SPIKE! I spiked it," she shouts.

"We get the point."

Eve throws the ball to Mo's dad.

It's Mo's dad's turn to serve.

He hits the ball over the net.

Ed's team hits it back.

Ed's team gets the point.

It's their turn to serve.

The ball goes from one

side of the net to the other.

At last it comes to Mo.

"Hit it! Hit it!"

Mo's father says.

Mo puts both hands together.

He hits the ball up.

Mo's father hits it to Eve.

She spikes it.

It's Mo's turn to serve.

He hits the ball high over the net.

The ball goes back and

forth until Eve's team

gets the point.

The game goes on.

The ball flies over Mo's head.

He wants to hit it.

He wants to spike it.

But he can't reach it.

He is the smallest

player in the game.

The score is 14–13.

"One more point," Eve says,

"and our team wins."

Mo is in the front row.

"Here it comes!"

Mo's dad says.

He dives to the sand.

He hits the ball

into the air.

"Hit it, Mo," Eve calls. "Spike it!"

Mo looks up but he

cannot see it.

The sun is in his eyes.

BAM! The ball hits Mo's head.

It bounces up and over the net.

It falls between two players

on Ed's team.

It hits the sand.

"Our point! Our point!"

Eve shouts.

"We win! We win!

Mo, you ARE a good-luck player."

"Let's go," Mo's dad says.

"Mom has a treat for us."

"This is a party," Mo's dad says,

"a volleyball party.

We played and Mo won the game."

"You did?" Mo's mom says.

Mo smiles. "The ball hit my head
and went back over the net.
It was the winning point."
"It was a lucky hit," his dad says,
"and Mo is a good-luck player."